Tightwad Tod

by Daphne Skinner
Illustrated by John Nez

The Kane Press
New York

Book Design/Art Direction: Roberta Pressel

Library of Congress Cataloging-in-Publication Data

Skinner, Daphne.
    Tightwad Tod / by Daphne Skinner ; illustrated by John Nez.
        p.   cm. — (Math matters.)
    Summary: Challenged to spend twenty dollars in one day, a boy who loves money not only learns about bargain hunting and keeping track of his remaining balance, he also learns that spending can be fun.
    ISBN 1-57565-109-2 (pbk. : alk. paper)
    [1. Subtraction—Fiction. 2. Money—Fiction.]
    I. Nez, John A., ill. II. Title. III. Series.
    PZ7+
    [Fic]—dc21

2001000852

10 9 8 7 6 5 4 3 2 1

First published in the United States of America in 2001 by The Kane Press.
Printed in Hong Kong.

Tod liked money. He liked getting his allowance. He liked getting birthday checks. Once he found a nickel on the street and it made him happy all day long.

Tod never spent his money. Whenever
he got some, he put it away. He had four
piggy banks, a penny jar, a money clip,
and a safe. They were all full.

One rainy Saturday Tod was counting his pennies when the phone rang.

"Tod! It's Jake!" called Tod's brother Ernest. "He's going to the movies. Do you want to go with him?"

"No, thanks," answered Tod. "I'm busy."

On Sunday Tod was putting quarters into paper wrappers when the phone rang.

"Tod! It's Jake!" said Ernest. "He's going to the park to play ball. Do you want to go?"

"Tell him no, thanks," answered Tod. "I'm busy."

On Monday Tod was folding dollar bills
into his money clip when the phone rang.

"Tod! Jake's riding his bike to the mall. Do
you want to go with him?" asked Ernest.

"No, thanks," answered Tod. "I'm busy."

"Tod," Ernest said, "I'm starting to worry about you. All you do is count your money."

Tod shrugged. He liked counting his money.

Ernest pulled a twenty-dollar bill out of his pocket. "Do you think you could spend one of these?" he asked.

"A twenty? Maybe," said Tod.

"Bet you couldn't," said Ernest. "You're too much of a tightwad."

"Bet I could," said Tod. He didn't like being called a tightwad.

"Then here's the twenty," said Ernest. "But if you don't spend all of it, you have to give it back, *plus* five dollars. Deal?"

"Deal," said Tod.

And then he called Jake.

On the way to the mall, Tod told Jake about the bet.

"Piece of cake!" said Jake. He liked to spend money.

They went to the pet store so Jake could buy fish food. "You could get something for Waldo here," Jake said. Waldo was Tod's dog.

Tod has

"How about this nylon bone?" asked Jake.

"I don't know," said Tod. "Three dollars is a lot of money. And they're not even real bones." He turned the twenty-dollar bill over and over in his hands.

"They're real nylon," said Jake.

"Well, okay," said Tod.

Tod pays with

His change is

They went to the bookstore next. Jake found a copy of *Mountain Bike* magazine. It cost $3.50.

"That's expensive," said Tod.

"But it has a story about biking in the Rockies," said Jake. "I'm going camping there this summer. I've got to get it."

Tod has

Tod saw a magazine called *Coin World*. It had stories about rare piggy banks, ancient coins, and the most valuable penny ever found. It cost $3.00. When Tod saw the price, he put *Coin World* back on the shelf. Then he picked it up again.

"Tod!" called Jake. "Come on!"

Tod bought the magazine.

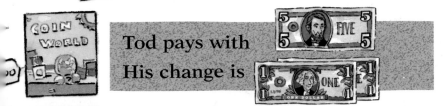

Tod pays with

His change is

"I could use a snack," said Jake.

"So could I," said Tod.

They stopped at the ice-cream store. Jake read the flavors. Tod read the prices.

"Mmmm! Chocolate Banana Gumbo," said Jake. He bought a cone.

Tod has

"$2.25 for a cone?" said Tod. "That's expensive."

"Not for Chocolate Banana Gumbo," said Jake. "Taste this," he said.

"Wow!" said Tod. He bought one, too.

Today's Flavor
Chocolate Banana Gumbo
$2.25

Tod pays with

His change is

They walked along eating their cones until they came to Bob's Bargains.

"Bob's has good stuff," said Jake. "Look at that Rocky Mountain calendar."

"It's last year's," said Tod. "I'll bet the pictures are nice, though."

"That's why I want it," said Jake.

Tod has

Then they noticed the calculators. Tod liked calculators. He spotted a solar calculator with musical buttons. "No batteries required!" he read. "Plays hundreds of tunes!"

"Cool!" said Jake. "Let's go in."

Tod bought it.

Tod pays with

His change is

Tod tried his new calculator on the up escalator. It made a chiming noise, like a tiny bell, and told him that he had $7.00 left to spend.

"Hey!" said Jake. "A sale at Happy Hats!"

Tod has

Beanies Drastically Reduced!

Golf Caps Low, Low Price!

Umbrella Hats 75% Off!

Jake tried on an umbrella hat. "I don't think so," said Tod.

Tod spotted a photo booth.

"Hmm. Four pictures for $3.00," he said.
He took out his new calculator. "That means
each picture costs 75 cents. Not bad."

Tod has

Tod took two pictures by himself.
Then Jake got in the booth with him,
and they took two more.

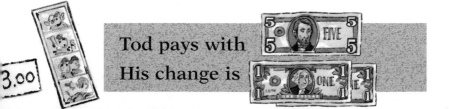

Tod pays with

His change is

21

On their way to the games arcade they stopped at The Gadgetorium. "Wow, an electronic money counter," said Tod.

"Perfect for you!" said Jake. "And it's only $9.95."

Tod counted his money. "I can't believe it," he said, "but I've only got $4 left. I wish I had enough money to buy—"

Tod has

"Tod! Am I glad to see you!" It was Ada, his next-door neighbor. "My mom asked me to buy cough drops, but I don't have enough money."

"I knew we shouldn't have bought those ice cream cones," said Ada's friend, Alison.

"Chocolate Banana Gumbo?" asked Jake.

The girls nodded. "So, can you lend me $2.00?" she asked.

"Sure," Tod said.

Tod lends Ada

"I'll pay you back tomorrow," Ada promised. "Thank you so much!"

"Hey! No problem," said Tod.

Tod has

"Let's go to the arcade before we run into anybody else," said Jake.

They played one game and another and another... until all Tod's money was gone.

"That was fun," said Tod. "And it went so fast! I'm broke." He grinned. "Wait till I tell Ernest!"

 Tod pays with

"Well, did you spend it all?" asked Ernest, when Tod got home.

"Yes," said Tod. "Look at all this stuff. I even loaned Alison $2.00."

"What? You did?" said Ernest.

"Well, she needed it," said Tod. "And she's paying me back. Docs that mean I lose the bet?"

"Not at all," said Ernest. "Lending is just as good as spending." He shook Tod's hand. "You win."

"So I'm not a tightwad," said Tod.

"Far from it," said Ernest.

The next day Tod went to the mall again on his way home from school.

"What's that?" asked Ernest, as Tod was heading upstairs.

"A money-counting machine," said Tod. "It works really fast."

"Wait a second," said Ernest. "You mean you're going to spend even more time counting your money?"

"No," said Tod. "I'm going to spend less time counting my money—and a lot *more* time having fun."

And he did!

USING MONEY CHART

Alison, Jake, and Tod go to the mall.

I have $3.00 left.

Alison buys:

$7.00

She pays with

Her change is:
Count on to $10.00

$7.00 → $8.00 →
$9.00 → $10.00

I have $1.25 left.

Jake buys:

$3.75

He pays with

His change is:
Count on to $5.00

$3.75 → $4.00 → $5.00

I have $.75 left.

Tod buys:

$2.25

He pays with

His change is:
Count on to $3.00

$2.25 → $2.50 → $3.00

8355